How the
RHINOCEROS
Got His Skin

For Hilary Thatcher,
Bosmere's "Best Beloved"
and never "Just So..."

Find out more about
Rudyard Kipling's
JUST SO STORIES
at Shoo Rayner's fabulous website,
www.shoo-rayner.co.uk

First published in 2007 by Orchard Books
First paperback publication in 2008

ORCHARD BOOKS
338 Euston Road, London NW1 3BH
Orchard Books Australia
Level 17/207 Kent St, Sydney, NSW 2000

ISBN 978 1 84616 402 6 (hardback)
ISBN 978 1 84616 410 1 (paperback)

Retelling and illustrations © Shoo Rayner 2007

1 3 5 7 9 10 8 6 4 2 (hardback)
1 3 5 7 9 10 8 6 4 2 (paperback)

Printed and bound in England by Antony Rowe Ltd, Chippenham, Wiltshire

Orchard Books is a division of Hachette Children's Books,
an Hachette Livre UK company.

www.orchardbooks.co.uk

Rudyard Kipling's
JUST SO STORIES

How the
RHINOCEROS
Got His Skin

Retold and illustrated by
SHOO RAYNER

ORCHARD BOOKS

Long, long ago, at the very beginning of time, when everything was just getting sorted out, there was a mostly uninhabited island on the shores of the Red Sea.

On the shore
of this island lived
a Man who was just
passing through.

He spent each day by the
Red Sea, wearing his hat, from which
the rays of the sun were reflected in
more-than-ornamental splendour.

Uninhabited Islands

Some uninhabited islands have nothing on them at all.

Some of them have palm trees growing on them.

Others have much more than palm trees growing on them but are still uninhabited.

Mostly uninhabited islands must be inhabited by *something*, so beware!

He had a cooking
stove that got hot on
the outside – one of
those stoves you must
never, ever touch.

One day he took flour and water and currants and plums and sugar and other delicious things, and made himself a cake.

It was twice as long across as it was deep, and as wide as his arms could circle.

It was indeed a Very Superior Comestible. He put it on the stove, because HE was allowed to, and he baked it and he baked it till it was all brown and smelt most mouthwateringly delectable.

Very superior comestibles

Comestible: item of food
Superior: high quality

If all you eat is cake, you had better
use only the best ingredients.

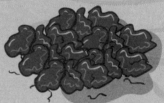

Plump, sweet
currants

Perfect purple
plums

Demerara
sugar

Candied peel

Champion
cherries

Organic eggs

Best butter

But just as he was going to eat it,
there came down to the beach from the
Altogether Uninhabited Interior a large
Rhinoceros with a horn on his nose, two
piggy eyes, and no manners.

In those days the Rhinoceros's skin fitted him quite tight. There were no wrinkles in it anywhere. He looked exactly like a toy Noah's Ark Rhinoceros, but of course much bigger.

The Altogether Uninhabited Interior

Nothing lives in the Altogether Uninhabited Interior.

But when the Rhinoceros is about, the Altogether Uninhabited Interior becomes the *Mostly* Uninhabited Interior.

The Rhinoceros had no manners then, and he has no manners now, and he never will have any manners to speak of. "Wa-how!" the Rhinoceros said.

"Wa-how!"

"Arrgh!" the Man screamed. He jumped up and ran away, leaving his cake behind.

He scrambled to the top
of a palm tree, still wearing
his hat, from which the rays
of the sun were reflected in
more-than-ornamental splendour.

The Rhinoceros humphed, and banged about in a most bad-mannered way. He knocked the stove over with his nose, and sent the cake rolling on the sand.

Then he spiked
that cake on the
horn of his nose,
and he ate it!

Waving his tail, the Rhinoceros trotted back to the desolate and Altogether Uninhabited Interior, which was a hop and a jump away from the islands of Mazanderan, Socotra, and the Promontories of the Larger Equinox.

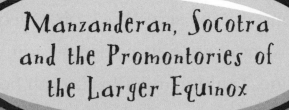

Manzanderan, Socotra and the Promontories of the Larger Equinox

Manzanderan and the Promontories of the Larger Equinox have moved south and can sometimes be found resting off the coast of Madagascar.

Socotra is home to the Dragon's Blood Tree, which bleeds dark red sap when scratched. The island is also a good place to find frankincense and myrrh.

The Man came down from his palm
tree and put the stove back on its legs.
He was not very happy, as you can well
imagine. Darkly, under his breath he
muttered a curse, which was more like
a rhyme than a verse:

Five weeks later, there
was a heat wave in the Red
Sea, and everybody took off
all the clothes they had.

The Man took
off his hat,

and the Rhinoceros took off his skin
and carried it over his shoulder as he
came down to the beach to bathe.

As he has never had any manners, nor ever will have any to speak of, the Rhinoceros said nothing at all about the Man's cake that he had gobbled up.

Now, in those days the Rhinoceros's skin buttoned underneath with three large buttons, making it look like a waterproof coat.

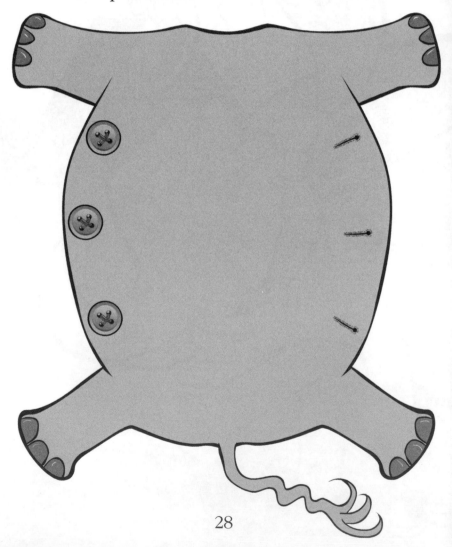

Leaving his skin on the
beach, he waddled straight
into the water and blew
bubbles through his nose.

When the Man came by, he found the skin, and he smiled a smile that ran all round his face two times.

Then he danced three
times round the skin and
rubbed his hands.

31

The Man went to his
camp and filled his hat
with cake-crumbs.

He never ate anything but
cake, and he never swept up
the crumbs from his table,

so his hat was
full to the brim.

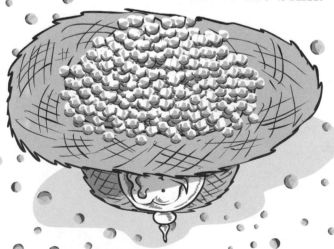

He took that skin, and he shook that skin, and he scrubbed that skin, and he rubbed that skin just as full of old, dry, stale, tickly cake-crumbs and some burnt currants as ever it could possibly hold.

Then he climbed to
the top of his palm
tree and waited for the
Rhinoceros to come
out of the water and
put his skin back on.

The Rhinoceros did just that. He buttoned it up with the three large buttons, and it tickled like cake-crumbs in bed!

The Rhinoceros wanted to scratch, but that made it worse. He lay down on the sand and rolled and rolled and rolled, and every time he rolled, the cake-crumbs tickled him worse and worse and worse.

39

Then he ran to the palm tree and rubbed and rubbed and rubbed himself against it. He rubbed so much and so hard that he rubbed his skin into a great fold over his shoulders,

and he rubbed
some more folds
over his legs,

and another fold underneath,
where the buttons used to be, but
he rubbed the buttons off!

41

He flew into a hot-headed rage, but it didn't make the least bit of difference to the cake-crumbs. They were inside his skin and they tickled.

So he stomped off home again, very
angry indeed and horribly scratchy.

The Man came down from his palm tree, and put on his hat, from which the rays of the sun were reflected in more-than-ornamental splendour.

He packed up his cooking stove, and took up his journey again, leaving in the direction of Orotavo, Amygdala, the Upland Meadows of Anantarivo, and the Marshes of Sonaput.

The Rhinoceros lived the
rest of his itchy, scratchy
life in the Altogether
Uninhabited Interior.

And from that day on, every
Rhinoceros had great folds in his skin
and a very bad temper, all on account
of the cake-crumbs inside.

Rudyard Kipling's

JUST SO STORIES

Retold and illustrated by

SHOO RAYNER

All priced at £8.99

Rudyard Kipling's Just So Stories are available from all good bookshops,
or can be ordered direct from
the publisher: Orchard Books, PO BOX 29, Douglas IM99 1BQ
Credit card orders please telephone 01624 836000
or fax 01624 837033 or visit our internet site: www.orchardbooks.co.uk
or e-mail: bookshop@enterprise.net for details.

To order please quote title, author and ISBN
and your full name and address.
Cheques and postal orders should be made payable to 'Bookpost plc.'
Postage and packing is FREE within the UK
(overseas customers should add £2.00 per book).

Prices and availability are subject to change.